SPEED UP, SAMMY THE TREE SLOTH!

WRITTEN BY CARL EMERSON

ILLUSTRATED BY ZACHARY TROVER

magic wagon

visit us at www.abdopublishing.com

Published by Magic Wagon, a division of the ABDO Publishing Group, 8000 West 78th Street, Edina, Minnesota, 55439.

Text by Carl Emerson
Illustrations by Zachary Trover
Edited by Nadia Higgins
Interior layout and design by Zachary Trover
Cover design by Zachary Trover

Printed in the United States.

Library of Congress Cataloging-in-Publication Data
Emerson, Carl.
  Speed up, Sammy the tree sloth! / Carl Emerson ; illustrated by Zachary Trover.
     p. cm. — (Animal underdogs)
  Summary: Sammy would rather hang from a branch all day than play with his monkey friends, but when a storm arrives,
it is his special ability that keeps his best friend safe.
   ISBN 978-1-60270-019-2
   [1. Sloths—Fiction. 2. Monkeys—Fiction. 3. Individuality—Fiction.] I. Trover, Zachary, ill. II. Title.
PZ7.E582Spe 2007
   [E]—dc22
                            2007006317

It was the kind of day that would make any monkey happy. Sunlight streamed through the treetops. A gentle breeze made the leaves whirr. All around, birds cackled and crowed and chirped.

The monkeys made good use of the brilliant day. All throughout the rain forest, they swung from branch to branch. They raced each other from one end of the trees to the other.

Mitch always won the monkey races. None of the other monkeys moved as quickly, swung as high, or screamed as loud as Mitch.

"Today I'm going to set a new record!" Mitch called to the other monkeys. "I'm going to make it from one end of the forest to the other, and I'm only going to touch five vines!"

All the other monkeys laughed. "No monkey could do that," one of them called.

"You'll see," Mitch shot back.

With that, he climbed higher than he ever had climbed before. Up, up to the top of the tallest tree Mitch went.

The rest of the monkeys grew quiet. They watched Mitch closely, curious to see what he was going to do.

At the top of the tree, Mitch grabbed the longest vine he could see. He clung on tightly. Then he shouted, "Here I go!"

With that, Mitch leaped off the tallest branch on the tallest tree. He swung down, down through the leaves and the vines. Just as it looked as if he would hit the ground, the vine straightened and bounced back. Mitch sprung back up into the air.

Mitch soared higher and higher. As the vine reached its highest point, Mitch let go. He reached for another vine and ...

Splat!

Mitch crashed into something furry. Whatever that furry thing was, it wasn't moving. Mitch fell hard to the ground below.

The monkey rubbed his head. "What WAS that?" he wondered.

Now all the other monkeys were howling with laughter. Mitch spat some hairs out of his mouth and climbed the tree to see what he had hit. Mitch didn't see anything at first. Finally, he saw something that looked very much like part of a tree, but also like his best friend.

"Sammy? Is that you?" Mitch asked.
"What are you doing over there?"

"Oh, you know," said Sammy the sloth. "I'm just hanging around."

"But Sammy," Mitch said, "didn't you see me coming?"

"Oh, yes, I did," Sammy said. "You were moving awfully fast. You were doing very well. It looked to me like you were going to make it. Until you hit me, that is."

Mitch's eyes grew wide. "Sammy, why didn't you move?"

"Oh, you know," Sammy said, "I like it right here."

Now even Mitch was laughing.

"Sammy, it's the most beautiful day in the whole world!" Mitch exclaimed. He danced from branch to branch as he spoke. "Why don't you move around a little and have some fun? You've stayed in the same place so long, you've got moss growing on your fur!"

"Aw, come on, Mitch," Sammy replied. "That's just me. I just like to hang around."

"Suit yourself," Mitch called as he bounced away. "I'm going to try to set another record!"

Late that night, when Mitch and the other monkeys were sound asleep, a strong wind shook the rain forest. The wind shook leaves from the trees.

Then it started to drizzle. Soon the drizzle turned into a steady rain. Finally, the wind and the rain turned into a raging monsoon!

The monkeys woke up and scattered in all directions. They scooted throughout the forest, warning their animal friends that it was time to take cover.

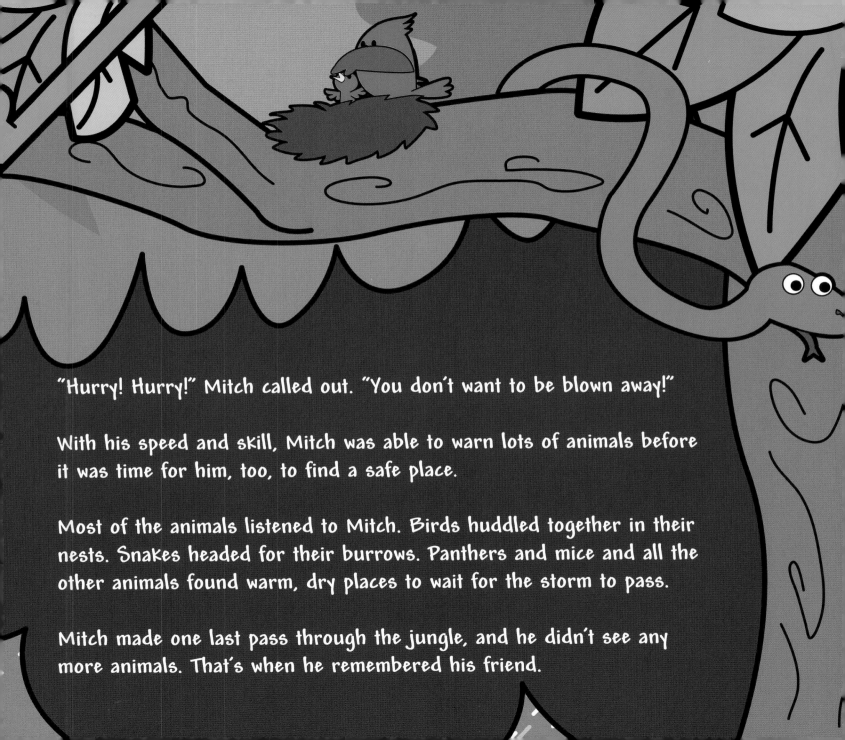

"Hurry! Hurry!" Mitch called out. "You don't want to be blown away!"

With his speed and skill, Mitch was able to warn lots of animals before it was time for him, too, to find a safe place.

Most of the animals listened to Mitch. Birds huddled together in their nests. Snakes headed for their burrows. Panthers and mice and all the other animals found warm, dry places to wait for the storm to pass.

Mitch made one last pass through the jungle, and he didn't see any more animals. That's when he remembered his friend.

Mitch spotted him. He swung through the trees, fighting against the wind, to reach Sammy.

Just as he got to Sammy, the wind grew even stronger.

"Sammy, this storm is very bad," Mitch said. "You've got to come down or you'll get knocked down."

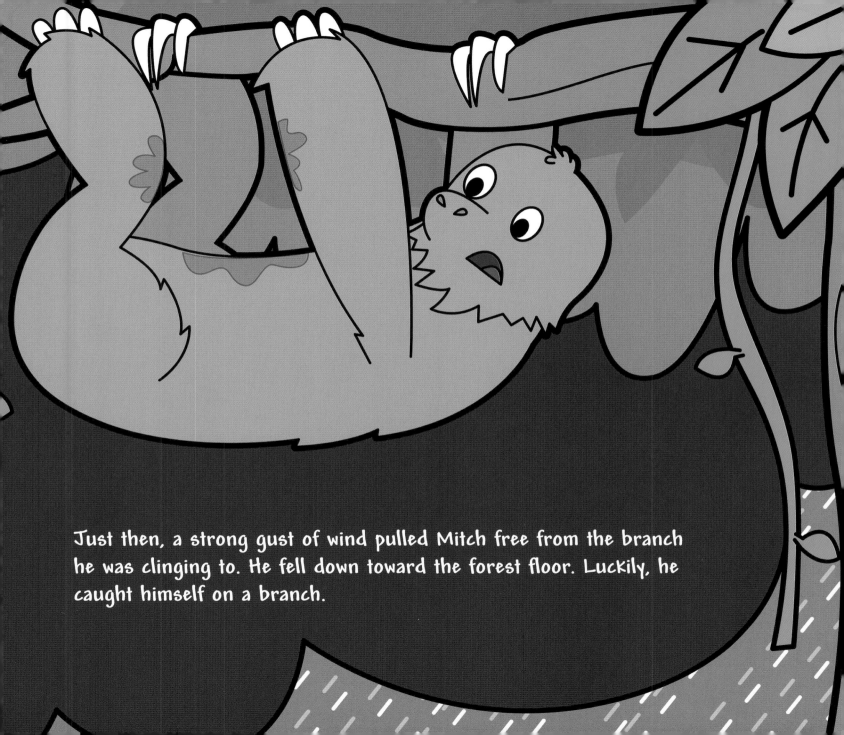

Just then, a strong gust of wind pulled Mitch free from the branch he was clinging to. He fell down toward the forest floor. Luckily, he caught himself on a branch.

In a flash, Mitch climbed back up to Sammy. Sammy swayed back and forth as the wind moved him.

"Sammy! Speed up! You have to move!" Mitch cried.

"I'm fine right here," Sammy said. "Maybe you should stay with me."

Mitch's forehead crinkled. "Stay in the trees? That's the worst place to be in a storm," he thought.

Then another mighty wind blew through the branches, and Mitch almost lost his grip again.

"Climb on," Sammy said to Mitch. "Let's hang around together!"

Mitch climbed onto Sammy's belly. "Will you be able to hold us both?" Mitch asked nervously.

"Oh, yes," Sammy said.
"My claws are very strong."

All night long, the storm raged.
The wind grew stronger.
The rain fell harder. Branches
were blown to the ground. But
all night long, Sammy clung to
the branch. And Mitch stayed
curled up on Sammy's belly,
safe and warm.

The next morning, the storm broke. Sunlight streamed through the branches again.

"You did it, Sammy!" Mitch yelped. "We made it through the storm!" Mitch climbed off Sammy's belly and stretched his arms.

"It's a beautiful day," Mitch said. "I think I'll try to set some new records! Want to come?"

"No, thanks," Sammy said. "I'm going to stay here and try to set my own record—to see how long I can hang from this branch!"

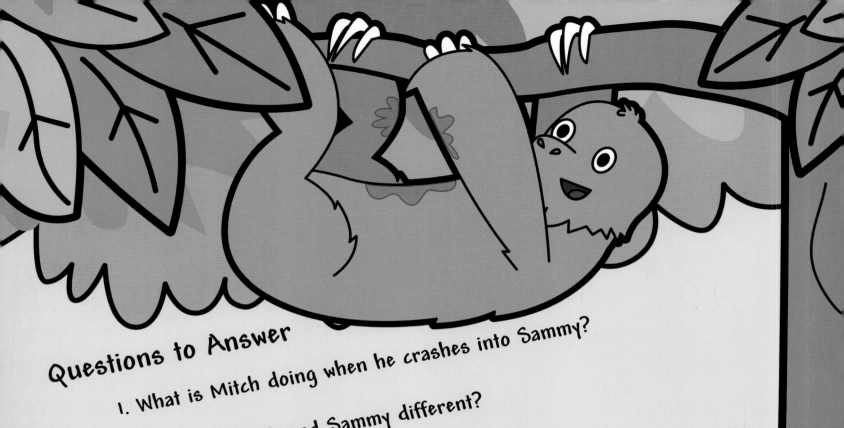

Questions to Answer

1. What is Mitch doing when he crashes into Sammy?

2. How are Mitch and Sammy different?

3. Where does Sammy like to hang out?

4. How does Mitch help his animal friends?

5. How does Sammy save the day?

6. What new record is Sammy trying to set?